Bloodlust

A letter to My Victims

Dante Remy
Concept & Author

Apollonia Saintclair
Illustrations

This book is a product of fiction. Any resemblance to real names, places, characters, or incidents is purely coincidental, as they are either the creation of the author's imagination or used fictitiously. All characters engaging in sexual activities within this work are portrayed as 18 years of age or older. Intended for **adult audiences**, this book contains sexually explicit scenes and explicit language that may be considered offensive by some readers. We encourage responsible reading and advise storing the book in a location inaccessible to minors.

Erosetti

Let us journey together

Erosetti | noun | : an interwoven art form of erotica, vignette, and media creating a captivating and intimate experience. A term coined to describe original works and collaborations with artists who share a passion for exploring the depths of human desire and sensuality.

Erosetti Press, LLC, is a niche publisher representing artists, writers, and creators who weave erotic, written, and visual media to create immersive audience experiences. Publishing print trade books and e-books, art prints, and limited-edition books, each publication is a journey into human desire and sensuality. *Let us journey together.*

Bloodlust
A Letter to My Victims

Discovery of the Bloodlust Story

During the turbulent days marking the fall of communism in Old Town Bratislava, an extraordinary discovery was made within the crumbling walls of an abandoned building. This structure, long neglected and veiled in the shadows of history, held secrets that would soon unravel a compelling narrative.

Urban explorers, driven by curiosity and the promise of forgotten relics, ventured into the building's eerie confines. Inside, they encountered blocked windows that once shut out the world, preserving the interior as a time capsule of a bygone era. The walls bore silent witness to years of political turmoil and societal change, their faded colors hinting at the lives that had unfolded within.

The most startling revelation came in the basement—a hidden grave. This underground resting place, shrouded in mystery, provided the final piece of a puzzle that had lain dormant for decades. Buried beneath layers of dust and decay was a collection writings and drawings, meticulously preserved and imbued with the essence of its clandestine origins.

Although we may never know her name, these documents tell a story that spans centuries and the history of a woman whose lust would not be denied. The Bloodlust manuscript, a testament to the enduring power of storytelling, is printed here for the first time. Written as a poetic letter, it captures a narrative that transcends its immediate context, weaving together the threads of psychosexual depravation and the need for meaning in existence. Was the author a vampire in the mythical sense, or predator feasting on human desire? The answer is for the reader to decide.

A manuscript page, found among notes and drawings.

In these pages, enter a world where ecstasy and agony intertwine, where the boundary between life and death blurs in a seductive dance of desire. *Bloodlust*, is a vampiric tale that delves into the darkest corners of human longing and the irresistible allure of the forbidden. Illustrated maps and images found alongside the manuscript, and artistic interpretation by the internationally acclaimed erotic artist Apollonia Saintclair, create an evocative layer to the sensual world of *Bloodlust*, told here for the first time.

Narrated in the mesmerizing voice of a centuries-old vampire, this story invites you to experience pleasure in its rawest form. The vampire is not merely a predator but a connoisseur, savoring the unique vintage of each victim's blood, enriched by their most intimate moments of release. As you turn each page, you'll be drawn into a narrative that is as much about the pursuit of orgasmic ecstasy as it is about the hunger for life itself.

One of the many mysterious maps and drawings
found among manuscript pages.

With each seduction, the vampire edges closer to the ultimate taste—blood flushed with the chemicals of climax, the purest expression of human desire. From the delicate flick of a tongue on tender skin to the fierce bite that drains life in a flood of passion, *Bloodlust* is an intoxicating journey through the senses. Prepare to be captivated by a story that explores the primal nature of lust and the intoxicating power of blood. This is a tale for those who dare to embrace their darkest fantasies and are willing to succumb to the seduction of *Bloodlust*.

The rediscovered manuscript of *Bloodlust* offers a unique blend of historical intrigue and erotic fantasy. As you delve into this volume, envision the lives that breathed within these pages. Picture the blocked windows, the whispers of a house that once harbored secrets, and the solemnity of the underground grave. This story, unearthed from the depths of history, invites you to witness a moment frozen in time—a poignant reminder of the tales that shape us and the power of discovery to illuminate our past and our most primal desires.

Dante Remy

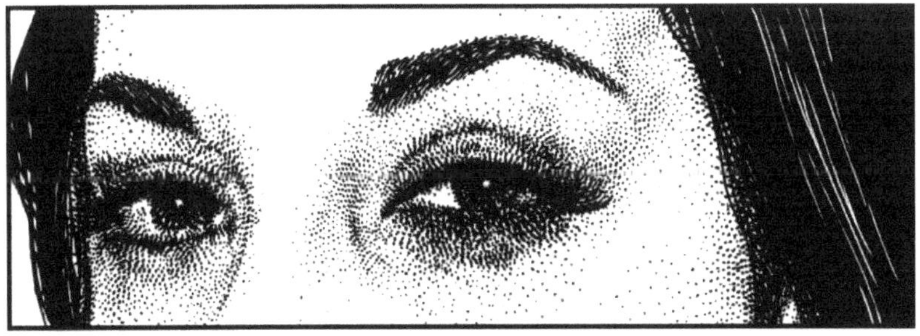

*Eyes of the narrator, as interpreted by the artist
Apollonia Saintclair.*

Bloodlust

Dante Remy

Bloodlust.
You are the vessel of my desire,
Seduced, kissed, touched,
Until your veins flow with the taste,
Of sex, and want, and need,
Until you beg for release,
Pleading for me to take you.

Most know me as a vampire,
An antihero of myth and legend,
Filled with foreboding and longing,
Filled with fear of what I am,
Of what I take,
Feeding to live,
Killing to exist.

I see myself as a connoisseur,
Marking two punctures just so,
Releasing a stream of life,
Pulsing with each beat,
Savoring nuances of taste,
Hints of eroticism,
The age, the vintage,
The...mmm...the ecstasy.

Your blood is my sex.

Centuries ago,
I would savor you slowly,
My tongue lightly flicking small cuts,
On the most erogenous parts of your body.
What is a pulsing, hard, cock,
If not a means for your pleasure,
And my taste?
Held in suspended need,
Your orgasm was the death of you.

I would spend entire evenings,
Edging and feeding on you:
The tip of my tongue,
Circling and tasting,
A small incision marking your arousal,
Pleasure washing over your fear and pain,
A red trickle covering hardened flesh.
Oh, how long you would endure my delight!

And, when I allowed you to cum?
You stood at the abyss of life,
Falling into shudders,
Pulsing,
Releasing an intoxicating mix,
Of hormones and blood chemicals,
Satisfying my bloodlust.
With the sweetest of vintages,
Directly to my being,
To my soul.

I would spend entire evenings, edging and feeding on you.

Blood can be wretched:
A foul meal of the pedestrian sort,
Polluted with processes,
Pharmaceuticals,
And the trash of human stress and storm.
I can smell a victim before I taste one.
However, it wasn't always this way.
I've learned to savor notes and overtones.

Each victim is a story in taste,
Carefully procured:
A dash of innocence,
A simple life,
Of curiosity.
Then, the hunt begins,
With an invitation to seduction.

My victims have ego and drive,
But not too much.
Just enough to make them curious,
And to appreciate the attention.
This vintage takes time:
Public but quietly living their life,
Social, yet solitary in their way.

It's not enough to find a victim.
This is the easy part.
Their aroma awakens me.
I patiently observe,
Senses heightened,
And record each subtle nuance:
Their likes and preferences;
Their appreciation of gestures;
Their desires, found in longing moments.

Most of all, my victims crave escape,
Escape from the mundane,
From the conventions of the everyday.
For the very reason I chose eternity,
My victims choose *la petite mort*:
A small death,
A release from life through pleasure,
Casting it all away to die in orgasm.

I become the one they wait for.
Subtle transformations wash across my body:
A hint of color here, height and eyes,
All their physical and behavioral desires,
Are internalized and change me,
Until I am obsessed,
And can have no one else...

But you.

Your orgasm is mine,
Procured to be enjoyed.
I feed on your most primitive pleasure center,
As endorphins wash away pain with pleasure,
Until the need to give yourself to me is
everything,
More than life,
And your blood is in its richest form,
Flush with oxytocin,
Our chemical bond.

But these are mere words of science.

Our desire is the study of lust.
Through the slow burn of arousal,
Blood becomes pleasure.
This is all you need to know:
Your blood allows me to experience eroticism.
Each taste of you brings me to the edge.

Bloodlust is pleasure,
In its most human form.
To perfect this vintage,
To truly drink your orgasm,
Would require assistance.
Why wait for pleasure to build,
When I could feast on it eternally?
Your orgasm,
Coursing through my veins,
For weeks,
Until my next victim.

This is when everything changed.
At first, I searched for couples,
Silently watching from a dark corner,
When their quiet gasp of ecstasy,
Triggered my impulse to strike,
Drinking through cries of pleasure,
Until a partner found a pale corpse.

There was so much to taste,
And I was annoyed with patience.
If I could seduce you,
Why couldn't others do so for me?
A seducer and seductress:
Assistants coupled to me,
Bringing me victims for my approval,
Like cats at a doorstep.

Bringing me victims for my approval, like cats at a doorstep.

Only the most vain would do.
These seducers,
Giving themselves to me,
Suckling them,
Teasing,
Encouraging their desire for immortality,
A growing bloodlust.
They would do anything for me,
Delivering victims was just the beginning.

Human turning on human,
Preparing the feast.

And you?
You join the chorus of victims,
So willing to give yourself over,
Trapped in a spiral of pleasure and discovery,
Savoring your seduction,
Begging through moans for more,
For release...
Allowing me to taste your ecstasy.

You are brought to me,
With promises of pleasure,
Curated,
Seduced,
Honored to be taken.
I hold you by the shoulders,
Caressing you into a trance,
As kisses make their way up your thighs,
Between your legs,
Turning your blood sweet.

Closer,
With tongue and lips,
I watch your eyes close,
As a sigh escapes your parted mouth.
Your head turns to the side,
Offering me your neck,
Giving up all pretense of control.
Your cock,
Beckoning for more,
But not yet.
The vintage is nearly perfect.

I feel your blood pulsing,
As the first kisses and touches of tongue,
Tease the length of your cock,
Engorged with the desire.
Hard and wanting,
A succulent stream of precum,
Falls to your tight balls,
Teasing the taste that awaits me,
Arousal,
Overtaking your body.

Yes, my love,
My passion,
My desire:
Call out the moans of centuries past,
From the place of primitive lust,
No words of meaning,
Your need expressed,
In breaths and sighs.
Sing your song of death.
Let the sounds of lust escape your mouth.

You are close now.
The long-haired head,
Teasing between your legs,
Is a vessel bringing me your pleasure.
Its steady rhythm picks up pace,
Pushing you further,
Only steadied by your hand,
Now gripping and bringing it closer to you,
Hair grasped between your fingers,
Forcing the mouth and tongue deeper...

Just right.

This is the moment:
Your veins full and beating,
Quicken the pulse across your neck,
Urging me to strike,
To take your orgasm,
As you orgasm for eternity,
Your moans calling to me,
To take you,
To release you.

My fangs strike deep.
My mouth surrounds the wounds,
My tongue moving back and forth,
Covering a mark momentarily,
Then, a warm pulse released,
Over and over,
Blood awash,
As your orgasm overtakes us.

Yes, cum for me.
Give me all of you.
Writhe and grip and dig your nails,
Forcing the warm mouth between your legs,
To give you pleasure,
As we drink all of you.
Cum! Cum for us!
Our bodies entwined in eternal ecstasy.

My moans vibrate against your neck,
As I struggle to devour you.
I grasp you tightly,
My body shaking,
My eyes rolling back,
Into this ancient rite.
Your orgasm consuming me..

Cumming...

Over, and over...

Each pulse,
Each beat,
A wave of orgasm,
As time fades away,
In our desire.

Pleasure.

Forever.

As your breath grows shallow,
We become one.
Shaking still in orgasm,
Your free hand reaches to pull me close,
Fixed in this pleasure,
Two mouths on you,
Cock and neck,
Keeping giver and taker close to you.

Your eyes open,
With the blank stare of fading life,
Freeing you with the knowledge,
In this final hour,
That this life-taking pleasure,
Is everything you have ever wanted.

Dying in orgasm is eternal bliss.

And you, my audience of victims?
You would give anything,
To return to this moment:
Edged beyond pain or reason,
Your desire for release all consuming,
Cumming as your life ends,
Your final orgasm,
The pinnacle of your existence.

Finally, at the end, knowing...

Bloodlust.

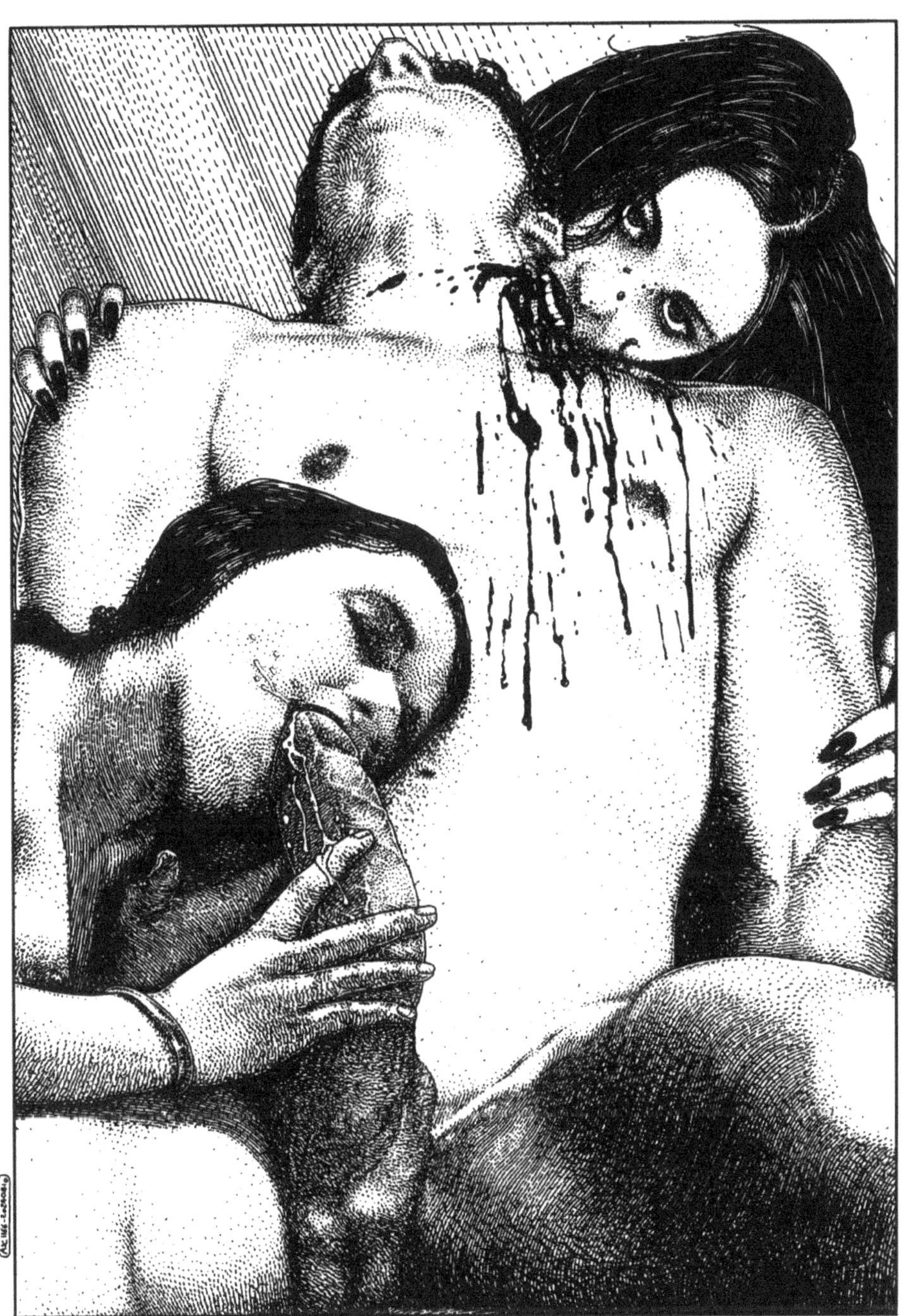

Your final orgasm, the pinnacle of your existence.

Bloodlust

The Story Continues

The trove of papers and illustrations found in Old Town Bratislava are revealing more stories. One manuscript of particular interest consists of notes and drawings about Carmilla, a young nun of the Convent of Poor Clares. Presently known as the Clarissine Church, a secular museum and event space, the mistress of these found works spent considerable time with Sister Carmilla in the stone walls of its main building, documenting events leading up to the late 1700s, when scandal led to the convent's closure. The notes reveal unholy trysts and scandalous rituals of blood and lust too detailed to retell here. The work to retell the stories of these texts as a novel continues, with a publication planned. A chapter will be dedicated to Carmilla.

The young nun Carmilla will serve as the focus of a chapter in the novel version of Bloodlust.

About the Author & Artist

 Dante Remy is an internationally-based writer, editor, and creator. His work explores the aesthetic in the everyday and the search for humanity through word, visualization, and soundscape. Running themes explore: the duality of nature and science, love and loss, beauty and the macabre, the chaste and the erotic. The Erosetti pillow book series marks his inaugural venture into published print erotica, seamlessly melding his distinct visual writing style with interpretations by skilled artists. His comprehensive portfolio can be explored at danteremy.com.

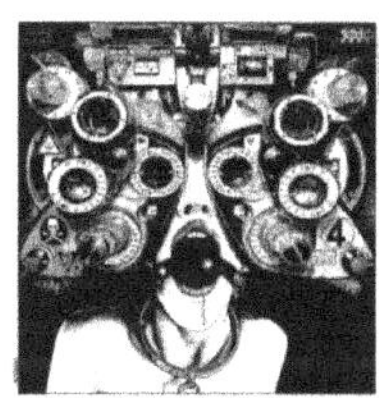 Apollonia Saintclair is a Geneva-based artist and self-taught illustrator with a tortuous past who draws for her pleasure and that of her audience. She also works for publishing houses, like the renown French erotic publisher La Musardine. Her imagination is fueled by Pop culture as well as academic canons and her graphic influences range from Leonardo da Vinci to Moebius and Milo Manara – among other European comic artists. She also finds great inspiration in The Silver Spoon. A longtime resident of the Old Continent, Apollonia divides her time between the kitchen and her workshop. Learn more about her art, her books, and projects at apolloniasaintclair.com.

Follow Us & Subscribe
ErosettiPress.com

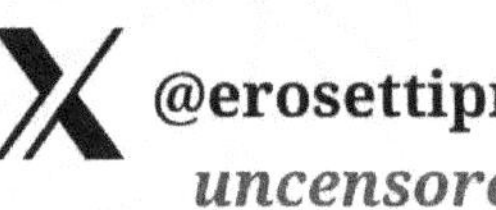

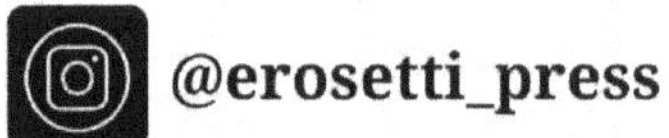

Podcasting on
all platforms!

Contemporary &
Classic Literature

Lover, Predator, Vampire
Blood and lust mingle with folklore in this new take on the vampire story, told in the voice of Milena, a heroine femme fatale ahead of her time.

The Mysteries,
I Misteri del Convento

A bold and transformative exploration of desire, faith, and surrender, blending historical erotica with spiritual awakening in a story that dares to illuminate the sacred power of the forbidden. Illustrated by world renown erotic artist Apollonia Saintclair.

Carmilla

The essential sapphic, erotic, vampire classic, now restored with the original serialized illustrations, period artwork, and a forward for curated reading experience.

Carmilla, My Love

The Vampire Speaks: The gothic classic told through the voice of the vampire, unbridled by Victorian restraint! Erotic. Sapphic. Bloodlust in sensuous detail.

Listen to Novels and Stories on the Erotica Obscura Podcast

Broadcasting on All Podcasting Platforms

Search "Erotica Obscura"

www.ingramcontent.com/pod-product-compliance
Lightning Source LLC
Chambersburg PA
CBHW040915010826
48978CB00013BB/1296